www.jilllorraineturpin.com

MY VERY OWN FIRE TRUCK

story and illustration
by

Jill Lorraine Turpin

For all my noisy boys.

This is my
fire truck,
shiny and new.
My very own
fire truck,

Do you have one too?

My fire truck has hoses,
that make a big splash,

and sirens and lights
that scream, blink, and flash.

I have a tall ladder
on my fire truck

to climb
up tall trees

and help cats that are stuck.

I rev up my engine
and drive really fast.

My friend
Zach was jealous
as I sped past.

Zach went to his mother
and cried lots of tears.

So he got a truck for
his birthday this year.

Zach and I
drove our trucks
all around town,

flashing and splashing
and making loud sounds.

But Pedro and Jenny,
and Marcus and Joan,
each wanted fire trucks
of their very own.

Soon we could never
find cats that were stuck,
because every house
had its own fire truck.

Our nice little town,
always quiet
before,

was filled
with the sounds
of sirens and roars.

We showed off our engines,
our lights, horns, and tires,
when all of a sudden
a house caught on fire!

No one had seen
a response so complete

as when thirty-six fire trucks
showed up on that street.

We all used our hoses.
They hit with a splat!

The fire was out in just
two seconds flat!

But before we could cheer
with a shout of "Hurray!"

we sprayed so much water
the house washed away!

So now in our town

all the girls
and the boys,

are only allowed to have

fire truck toys.

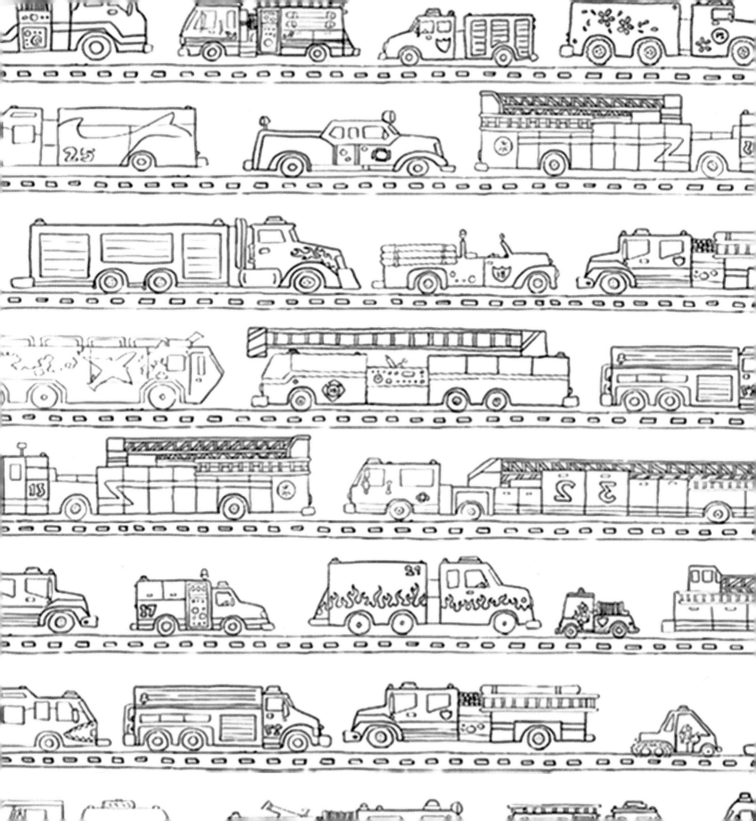

45032861R00022

Made in the USA
San Bernardino, CA
24 July 2019